Ribbon Rescue

Robert Munsch

Ribbon Rescue

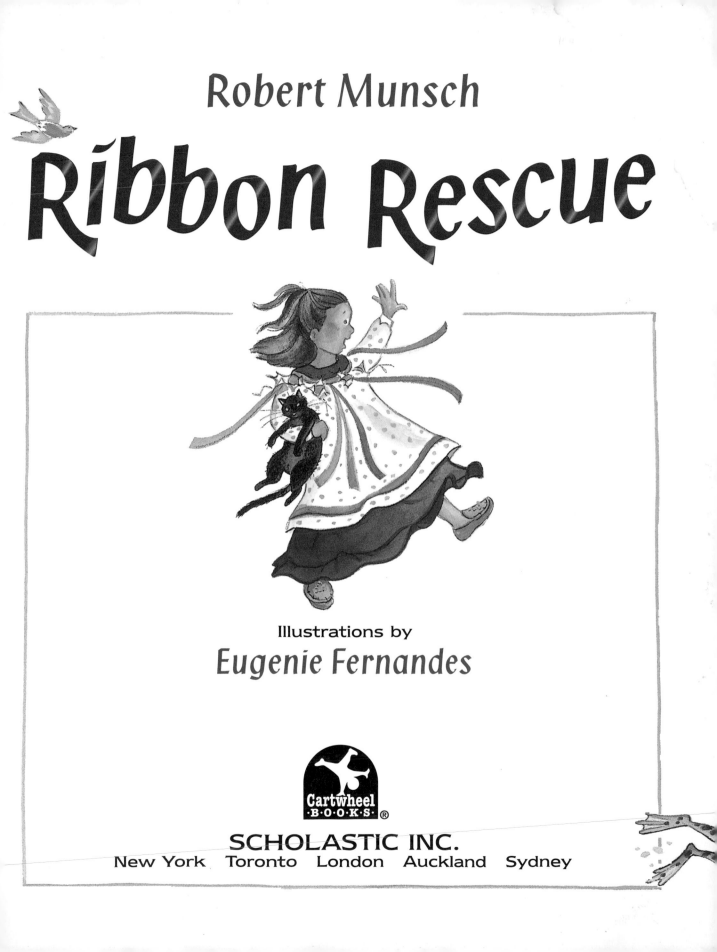

Illustrations by
Eugenie Fernandes

Cartwheel
·B·O·O·K·S·®

SCHOLASTIC INC.
New York   Toronto   London   Auckland   Sydney

The paintings for this book were created in gouache and colored pencils
on Arches Water Color Paper.

This book was designed in QuarkXPress, with type set in 18 point Poppl-Pontifex.

Library of Congress Cataloging-in-Publication Data
Munsch, Robert N., 1945 –
     Ribbon rescue / by Robert Munsch ; illustrated by Eugenie Fernandes.
          p.   cm.
     "Cartwheel Books."
     Summary: A young girl unselfishly gives away the ribbons from her new dress to
help various people on their way to a wedding.
     ISBN 0-590-89012-3
     [1. Ribbons–Fiction. 2. Weddings–Fiction. 3. Generosity–Fiction.] I. Fernandes,
Eugenie, ill. II. Title.
PZ7.M927R1 1999
[E]–dc21
                                                                                    98-30655
                                                                                    CIP
                                                                                    AC

10 9 8 7 6 5 4 3 2 1   Printed in Canada   9 /9 0/0 01 02 03 04
                                           First printing, May 1999

For Jillian DeLaronde
Kahnawake, Quebec.
—R.M.

For Robyn,
Julia,
Alexandra
and Katherine.
—E.F.

As soon as her grandmother finished making the ribbon dress, Jillian put it on and ran out into the front yard.

A man came running down the road.
He was dressed in fancy clothes and
he was yelling:
　"I'm late, I'm lost!
　I'm late, I'm lost!
　I'm going to miss my own wedding."
　"Wait," said Jillian. "Let me fix your shoes."
She tore two ribbons off her dress, laced
the man's shoes with them, and tied them
into big bows.

The man said, "Thanks. I may be late, but I'll look fine."

"Well," said Jillian, "why don't you take my brother Lewis's skateboard. He is grown up and doesn't use it anymore. Just keep your eye on the church steeple and you will get there."

"Thank you," said the man. "I'll bring it back as soon as the wedding is over."

Then a lady in a fancy white dress came running by.
She was yelling:

"I'm late, I'm lost!

I'm late, I'm lost!

I'm going to miss my own wedding."

"Well," said Jillian, "at least I can fix your hair."

Jillian reached up and tore eight ribbons off her
dress: one, two, three, four, five, six, seven, eight. Then
the lady bent down and Jillian fixed her hair into four
enormous ponytails.

"And now," said Jillian, "take my mother's bicycle. She is grown up and doesn't use it very much. Just keep heading for the church steeple and you will be there in no time."

"Oh, thank you," said the lady. "I might be late, but at least I will look okay." She gave Jillian a hug and rode away on the bicycle.

Then a family came running down the road yelling,
"We're late. We're lost!
We're late. We're lost!
We're going to miss the wedding.
We haven't even had time to wrap the present."
"Well," said Jillian, "I can wrap your present."
And she wrapped the present with five ribbons
from her dress.

The family said, "Oh, thank you. Thank you. Thank you. Thank you. We may be late, but we will have a lovely present."

"And now," said Jillian, "take Lindsay's wagon and Hayley's scooter. They are sort of grown up and don't use them very much. Just keep heading for the church steeple and you will not get lost."

They all gave Jillian a hug and raced off.

Then a man came down the road yelling,
"I'm late. I'm lost!
I'm late. I'm lost!
I'm going to miss the wedding."
Suddenly he stopped and said, "Oh, NO! It's lost!"
"What's lost?" said Jillian.
"The ring! The wedding ring!" said the man.
"I've lost the ring."
"I'll help you find it," said Jillian.
She crawled around and got quite dirty, but after
a while she found the ring in a mud puddle.

"Look," said Jillian, "you might lose it again.
Let me help you."

She tied the ring to the man's finger with
a ribbon.

"And now," said Jillian, "take Jeremy's skates.
He is grown up and doesn't use them very
much. Just keep heading for the church steeple."

"Thank you," said the man. "I may be late,
but at least I'll have the ring."

Then Jillian's mother came running out
of the house, yelling, "Jillian, we're late for a
wedding and you're a mess. What will your
grandmother say?"

She grabbed Jillian's hand and they ran
down the road.

But when they got to the church the man at the door said to Jillian, "What a mess! You can't come in here dressed like that!"

"But, but . . . ," said her mother.

"That's okay," said Jillian. "I will sit on the stairs and wait for you."

Then the bride and groom walked around the side of the church and saw Jillian sitting on the stairs.

"Oh," said the groom. "Don't my shoes look great?"

"Oh," said the bride. "Isn't my hair wonderful?"

"Yes," said Jillian. "Your shoes are great and your hair is wonderful and I hope you have a wonderful wedding."

"Aren't you coming in?" said the groom.

"No," said Jillian, "I tore off all my ribbons to fix hair, lace shoes, wrap a present, and tie a ring. Now my dress is a mess and I can't come in."

"Hhhhuuummm," said the groom. "I think we need a flower girl."

"Hhhhuuummm," said the bride. "Yes, we definitely need a flower girl."

So they picked a bunch of wildflowers from the grass and Jillian walked into the church in front of everybody else.

And even though her dress was all dirty and full of holes, everyone said she was the prettiest kid there.

Jillian is a Mohawk from the Kahnawake reserve near Montreal, Quebec. Her ribbon dress is a traditional Mohawk costume.